THE QUEER STORY
OF
BROWNLOW'S NEWSPAPER

By

H. G. WELLS

British Library Cataloguing-in-Publication Data
A catalogue record for this book is available from
the British Library

CONTENTS

H. G. WELLS

Herbert George Wells was born in Bromley, England in 1866. He apprenticed as a draper before becoming a pupil-teacher at Midhurst Grammar School in West Sussex. Some years later, Wells won a scholarship to the School of Science in London, where he developed a strong interest in biology and evolution, founding and editing the *Science Schools Journal*. However, he left before graduating to return to teaching, and began to focus increasingly on writing. His first major essay on science, 'The Rediscovery of the Unique', appeared in 1891. However, it was in 1895 that Wells seriously established himself as a writer, with the publication of the now iconic novel, *The Time Machine*.

Wells followed *The Time Machine* with the equally well-received *War of the Worlds* (1898), which proved highly popular in the USA, and was serialized in the magazine *Cosmopolitan*. Around the turn of the century, he also began to write extensively on politics, technology and the future, producing works *The Discovery of the Future* (1902) and *Mankind in the Making* (1903). An active socialist, in 1904 Wells joined the Fabian Society, and his 1905 book *A Modern Utopia* presented a vision of a socialist society founded on reason and compassion. Wells also penned a range of successful comic novels, such as *Kipps* (1905) and *The History of Mr Polly* (1910).

Wells' 1920 work, *The Outline of History,* was penned in response to the Russian Revolution, and declared that world would be improved by education, rather than revolution. It made Wells one of the most important political thinkers of the twenties and thirties, and he began to write for a number of journals and newspapers, even travelling to Russia to lecture Lenin and Trotsky on social reform. Appalled by the carnage of World War II, Wells began to work on a project dealing with the perils of nuclear war, but died before completing it. He is now regarded as one of the greatest science-fiction writers of all time, and an important political thinker.

§ 1

I call this a Queer Story because it is a story without an explanation. When I first heard it, in scraps, from Brownlow I found it queer and incredible. But—it refuses to remain incredible. After resisting and then questioning and scrutinizing and falling back before the evidence, after rejecting all his evidence as an elaborate mystification and refusing to hear any more about it, and then being drawn to reconsider it by an irresistible curiosity and so going through it all again, I have been forced to the conclusion that Brownlow, so far as he can tell the truth, has been telling the truth. But it remains queer truth, queer and exciting to the imagination. The more credible his story becomes the queerer it is. It troubles my mind. I am fevered by it, infected not with germs but with notes of interrogation and unsatisfied curiosity.

Brownlow is, I admit, a cheerful spirit. I have known him tell lies. But I have never known him do anything so elaborate and sustained as this affair, if it is a mystification, would have to be. He is incapable of anything so elaborate and sustained. He is too lazy and easy-going for anything of the sort. And he would have laughed. At some stage he would have laughed and given the whole thing away. He has nothing to gain by keeping it up. His honour is not in the case either way. And after all there is his bit of newspaper in evidence—and the scrap of an addressed wrapper. ...

I realize it will damage this story for many readers that it opens with Brownlow in a state very definitely on the gayer side of sobriety. He was not in a mood for cool and calculated observation, much less for accurate record. He was seeing things in an exhilarated manner. He was disposed to see them and greet them cheerfully and let them slip by out of attention. The limitations of time and space lay lightly upon him. It was after midnight. He had been dining with friends.

I have inquired what friends—and satisfied myself upon one or two obvious possibilities of that dinner party. They were, he said to me, "just friends. They hadn't anything to do with it." I don't usually push past an assurance of this sort, but I made an exception in this case. I watched my man and took a chance of repeating the question. There was nothing out of the ordinary about that dinner party, unless it was the fact that it was an unusually good dinner party. The host was Redpath Baynes, the solicitor, and the dinner was in his house in St. John's Wood. Gifford, of the *Evening Telegraph*, whom I know slightly, was, I found, present, and from him I got all I wanted to know. There was much bright and discursive talk and Brownlow had been inspired to give an imitation of his aunt, Lady Clitherholme, reproving an inconsiderate plumber during some re-building operations at Clitherholme. This early memory had been received with considerable merriment—he was always very good about his aunt, Lady Clitherholme—and Brownlow had departed obviously elated by this little social success and the general geniality of the occasion. Had they talked, I asked, about the Future, or Einstein, or J.W. Dunne, or any such high and serious topic at that party? They had not. Had they discussed the modern newspaper? No. There had been nobody whom one could call a practical joker at this party, and Brownlow had gone off alone in a taxi. That is what I was most desirous of knowing. He had been duly delivered by his taxi at the main entrance to Sussex Court.

Nothing untoward is to be recorded of his journey in the lift to the fifth floor of Sussex Court. The liftman on duty noted nothing exceptional. I asked if Brownlow said, "Good night." The liftman does not remember. "Usually he says Night O," reflected the liftman—manifestly doing his best and with nothing particular to recall. And there the fruits of my inquiries about the condition of Brownlow on this particular evening conclude. The rest of the story comes directly from him. My investigations arrive only at this: he was certainly not drunk. But he was lifted a little out of our normal harsh and grinding contact with the immediate realities of existence. Life was glowing softly and warmly in him, and the unexpected could happen brightly, easily, and acceptably.

He went down the long passage with its red carpet, its clear light, and its occasional oaken doors, each with its artistic brass number. I have been down that passage with him on several occasions. It was his custom to enliven that corridor by raising his hat gravely as he passed each entrance, saluting his unknown and invisible neighbours, addressing them softly but distinctly by playful if sometimes slightly indecorous names of his own devising, expressing good wishes or paying them little compliments.

He came at last to his own door, number 49, and let himself in without serious difficulty. He switched on his hall light. Scattered on the polished oak floor and invading his Chinese carpet were a number of letters and circulars, the evening's mail. His parlourmaid-housekeeper who slept in a room in another part of the building, had been taking her evening out, or these letters would have been gathered up and put on the desk in his bureau. As it was, they lay on the floor. He closed his door behind him or it closed of its own accord; he took off his coat and wrap, placed his hat on the head of the Greek charioteer whose bust adorns his hall, and set himself to pick up his letters.

This also he succeeded in doing without misadventure. He was a little annoyed to miss the *Evening Standard*. It is his custom, he says, to subscribe for the afternoon edition of the Star to read at tea-time and also for the final edition of the *Evening Standard* to turn over the last thing at night, if only on account of Low's cartoon. He gathered up all these envelopes and packets and took them with him into his little sitting-room. There he turned on the electric heater, mixed himself a weak whisky-and-soda, went to his bedroom to put on soft slippers and replace his smoking jacket by a frogged jacket of llama wool, returned to his sitting-room, lit a cigarette, and sat down in his arm-chair by the reading lamp to examine his correspondence. He recalls all these details very exactly. They were routines he had repeated scores of times.

Brownlow's is not a preoccupied mind; it goes out to things. He is one of those buoyant extroverts who open and read all their letters and circulars whenever they can get hold of them. In the daytime his secretary intercepts and deals with most of them, but at night he escapes from her control and does what he pleases, that is to say, he opens everything.

He ripped up various envelopes. There was a formal acknowledgment of a business letter he had dictated the day before, there was a letter from his solicitor asking for some details about a settlement he was making, there was an offer from some unknown gentleman with an aristocratic name to lend him money on his note of hand alone, and there was a notice about a proposed new wing to his club. "Same old stuff," he sighed. "Same old stuff. What bores they all are!" He was always hoping, like every man who is proceeding across the plains of middle-age, that his correspondence would contain agreeable surprises—and it never did. Then, as he put it to me, *inter alia*, he picked up the remarkable newspaper.

§ 2

It was different in appearance from an ordinary newspaper, but not so different as not to be recognizable as a newspaper, and he was surprised, he says, not to have observed it before. It was enclosed in a wrapper of pale green, but it was unstamped; apparently it had been delivered not by the postman, but by some other hand. (This wrapper still exists; I have seen it.) He had already torn it off before he noted that he was not the addressee.

For a moment or so he remained looking at this address, which struck him as just a little odd. It was printed in rather unusual type: "Evan O'Hara Mr., Sussex Court 49."

"Wrong name," said Mr. Brownlow; "Right address. Rummy. Sussex Court 49. ... 'Spose he's got my Evening Standard. ... 'Change no robbery."

He put the torn wrapper with his unanswered letters and opened out the newspaper.

The title of the paper was printed in large slightly ornamental black-green letters that might have come from a kindred fount to that responsible for the address. But, as he read it, it was the *Evening Standard!* Or, at least, it was the "Even Standrd." "Silly," said Brownlow. "It's some damn Irish paper. Can't spell—anything—these Irish. ..."

He had, I think, a passing idea, suggested perhaps by the green wrapper and the green ink, that it was a lottery stunt from Dublin.

Still, if there was anything to read he meant to read it. He surveyed the front page. Across this ran a streamer headline: "Wilton Boring reaches Seven Miles: Succes Assured."

"No," said Brownlow. "It must be oil. ... Illiterate lot these oil chaps—leave out the 's' in 'success.'"

He held the paper down on his knee for a moment, reinforced himself by a drink, took and lit a second cigarette, and then leant back in his chair to take a dispassionate view of any oil-share pushing that might be afoot.

But it wasn't an affair of oil. It was, it began to dawn upon him, something stranger than oil. He found himself surveying a real evening newspaper, which was dealing, so far as he could see at the first onset, with the affairs of another world.

He had for a moment a feeling as though he and his arm-chair and his little sitting-room were afloat in a vast space and then it all seemed to become firm and solid again.

This thing in his hands was plainly and indisputably a printed newspaper. It was a little odd in its letterpress, and it didn't feel or rustle like ordinary paper, but newspaper it was. It was printed in either three or four columns—for the life of him he cannot remember which—and there were column headlines under the page streamer. It had a sort of art-nouveau affair at the bottom of one column that might be an advertisement (it showed a woman in an impossibly big hat), and in the upper left-hand corner was an unmistakable weather chart of Western Europe, with *coloured* isobars, or isotherms, or whatever they are, and the inscription: "To-morrow's Weather."

And then he remarked the date. The date was November 10th, 1971!

"Steady on," said Brownlow. "Damitall! Steady on."

He held the paper sideways, and then straight again. The date remained November 10th, 1971.

He got up in a state of immense perplexity and put the paper down. For a moment he felt a little afraid of it. He rubbed his forehead. "Haven't been doing a Rip Van Winkle, by any chance, Brownlow, my boy?" he said. He picked up the paper again, walked out into his hall and looked at himself in the hall mirror. He was reassured to see no signs of advancing age, but the expression of mingled consternation and amazement upon his flushed face struck him suddenly as being undignified and unwarrantable. He laughed at himself, but not uncontrollably. Then he stared blankly at that familiar countenance. "I must be half-way *tordu*" he said, that being his habitual facetious translation of "screwed." On the console table was a little respectable-looking adjustable calendar bearing witness that the date was November 10th, 1931.

"D'you see?" he said, shaking the queer newspaper at it reproachfully. "I ought to have spotted you for a hoax ten minutes ago. 'Moosing trick, to say the least of it. I suppose they've made Low editor for a night, and he's had this idea. Eh?"

He felt he had been taken in, but that the joke was a good one. And, with quite unusual anticipations of entertainment, he returned to his arm-chair. A good idea it was, a paper forty years ahead. Good fun if it was well done. For a time nothing but the sounds of a newspaper being turned over and Brownlow's breathing can have broken the silence of the flat.

§ 3

Regarded as an imaginative creation, he found the thing almost too well done. Every time he turned a page he expected the sheet to break out into laughter and give the whole thing away. But it did nothing of the kind. From being a mere quip, it became an immense and amusing, if perhaps a little over-elaborate, lark. And then, as a lark, it passed from stage to stage of incredibility until, as any thing but the thing it professed to be, it was incredible altogether. It must have cost far more than an ordinary number. All sorts of colours were used, and suddenly he came upon illustrations that went beyond amazement; they were in the colours of reality. Never in all his life had he seen such colour printing—and the buildings and scenery and costumes in the pictures were strange. Strange and yet credible. They were colour photographs of actuality forty years from now. He could not believe anything else of them. Doubt could not exist in their presence.

His mind had swung back, away from the stunt-number idea altogether. This paper in his hand would not simply be costly beyond dreaming to produce. At any price it could not be produced. All this present world could not produce such an object as this paper he held in his hand. He was quite capable of realizing that.

He sat turning the sheet over and—quite mechanically—drinking whisky. His sceptical faculties were largely in suspense; the barriers of criticism were down. His mind could now accept the idea that he was reading a newspaper of forty years ahead without any further protest.

It had been addressed to Mr. Evan O'Hara, and it had come to him. Well and good. This Evan O'Hara evidently knew how to get ahead of things. ...

I doubt if at that time Brownlow found anything very wonderful in the situation.

Yet it was, it continues to be, a very wonderful situation. The wonder of it mounts to my head as I write. Only gradually have I been able to build up this picture of Brownlow turning over that miraculous sheet, so that I can believe it myself. And you will understand how, as the thing flickered between credibility and incredibility in my mind, I asked him, partly to justify or confute what he told me, and partly to satisfy a vast expanding and, at last, devouring curiosity: "What was there in it? What did it have to say?" At the same time, I found myself trying to catch him out in his story, and also asking him for every particular he could give me.

What was there in it? In other words, What will the world be doing forty years from now? That was the stupendous scale of the vision, of which Brownlow was afforded a glimpse. The world forty years from now! I lie awake at nights thinking of all that paper might have revealed to us. Much it did reveal, but there is hardly a thing it reveals that does not change at once into a constellation of riddles. When first he told me about the thing I was—it is, I admit, an enormous pity—intensely sceptical. I asked him questions in what people call a "nasty" manner. I was ready—as my manner made plain to him—to jump down his throat with "But that's preposterous!" at the very first slip.

And I had an engagement that carried me off at the end of half an hour. But the thing had already got hold of my imagination, and I rang up Brownlow before tea-time, and was biting at this "queer story" of his again. That afternoon he was sulking because of my morning's disbelief, and he told me very little. "I was drunk and dreaming, I suppose," he said. "I'm beginning to doubt it all myself." In the night it occurred to me for the first time that, if he was not allowed to tell and put on record what he had seen, he might become both confused and sceptical about it himself. Fancies might mix up with it. He might hedge and alter to get it more credible. Next day, therefore, I lunched and spent the afternoon with him, and arranged to go down into Surrey for the week-end. I managed to dispel his huffiness with me. My growing keenness restored his. There we set ourselves in earnest, first of all to recover everything he could remember about his newspaper and then to form some coherent idea of the world about which it was telling.

It is perhaps a little banal to say we were not trained men for the job. For who could be considered trained for such a job as we were attempting? What facts was he to pick out as important and how were they to be arranged? We wanted to know everything we could about 1971; and the little facts and the big facts crowded on one another and offended against each other.

The streamer headline across the page about that seven-mile Wilton boring, is, to my mind, one of the most significant items in the story. About that we are fairly clear. It referred, says Brownlow, to a series of attempts to tap the supply of heat beneath the surface of the earth. I asked various questions. "It was *explained*, y'know," said Brownlow, and smiled and held out a hand with twiddling fingers. "It was explained all right. Old system, they said, was to go down from a few hundred feet to a mile or so and bring up coal and burn it. Go down a bit deeper, and there's no need to bring up and burn anything. Just get heat itself straightaway. Comes up of its own accord—under its own steam. See? Simple.

"They were making a big fuss about it," he added. "It wasn't only the streamer headline; there was a leading article in big type. What was it headed? Ah! The Age of Combustion has Ended!"

Now that is plainly a very big event for mankind, caught in mid-happening, November 10th, 1971. And the way in which Brownlow describes it as being handled, shows clearly a world much more preoccupied by economic essentials than the world of to-day, and dealing with them on a larger scale and in a bolder spirit.

That excitement about tapping the central reservoirs of heat, Brownlow was very definite, was not the only symptom of an increase in practical economic interest and intelligence. There was much more space given to scientific work and to inventions than is given in any contemporary paper. There were diagrams and mathematical symbols, he says, but he did not look into them very closely because he could not get the hang of them. "*Frightfully* highbrow, some of it," he said.

A more intelligent world for our grandchildren evidently, and also, as the pictures testified, a healthier and happier world.

"The fashions kept you looking," said Brownlow, going off at a tangent, "all coloured up as they were."

"Were they elaborate?" I asked.

"Anything *but*" he said.

His description of these costumes is vague. The people depicted in the social illustrations and in the advertisements seemed to have reduced body clothing—I mean things like vests, pants, socks and so forth—to a minimum. Breast and chest went bare. There seem to have been tremendously exaggerated wristlets, mostly on the left arm and going as far up as the elbow, provided with gadgets which served the purpose of pockets. Most of these armlets seem to have been very decorative, almost like little shields. And then, usually, there was an immense hat, often rolled up and carried in the hand, and long cloaks of the loveliest colours and evidently also of the most beautiful soft material, which either trailed from a sort of gorget or were gathered up and wrapped about the naked body, or were belted up or thrown over the shoulders.

There were a number of pictures of crowds from various parts of the world. "The people looked fine," said Brownlow. "Prosperous, you know, and upstanding. Some of the women—just lovely."

My mind went off to India. What was happening in India?

Brownlow could not remember anything very much about India. "Ankor," said Brownlow. "That's not India, is it?" There had been some sort of Carnival going on amidst "perfectly lovely" buildings in the sunshine of Ankor.

The people there were brownish people but they were dressed very much like the people in other parts of the world.

I found the politician stirring in me. Was there really nothing about India? Was he sure of that? There was certainly nothing that had left any impression in Brownlow's mind. And Soviet Russia? "Not as Soviet Russia," said Brownlow. All that trouble had ceased to be a matter of daily interest. "And how was France getting on with Germany?" Brownlow could not recall a mention of either of these two great powers. Nor of the British Empire as such, nor of the U.S.A. There was no mention of any interchanges, communications, ambassadors, conferences, competitions, comparisons, stresses, in which these governments figured, so far as he could remember. He racked his brains. I thought perhaps all that had been going on so entirely like it goes on to-day—and has been going on for the last hundred years—that he had run his eyes over the passages in question and that they had left no distinctive impression on his mind. But he is positive that it was not like that. "All that stuff was washed out," he said. He is unshaken in his assertion that there were no elections in progress, no notice of Parliament or politicians, no mention of Geneva or anything about armaments or war. All those main interests of a contemporary journal seem to have been among the "washed out" stuff. It isn't that Brownlow didn't notice them very much; he is positive they were not there.

Now to me this is a very wonderful thing indeed. It means, I take it, that in only forty years from now the great game of sovereign states will be over. It looks also as if the parliamentary game will be over, and as if some quite new method of handling human affairs will have been adopted. Not a word of patriotism or nationalism; not a word of party, not an allusion. But in only forty years! While half the human beings already alive in the world will still be living! You cannot believe it for a moment. Nor could I, if it wasn't for two little torn scraps of paper. These, as I will make clear, leave me in a state of—how can I put it?— incredulous belief.

§ 4

After all, in 1831 very few people thought of railway or steamship travel, and in 1871 you could already go round the world in eighty days by steam, and send a telegram in a few minutes to nearly every part of the earth. Who would have thought of that in 1831? Revolutions in human life, when they begin to come, can come very fast. Our ideas and methods change faster than we know.

But just forty years!

It was not only that there was this absence of national politics from that evening paper, but there was something else still more fundamental. Business, we both think, finance that is, was not in evidence, at least upon anything like contemporary lines. We are not quite sure of that, but that is our impression. There was no list of Stock Exchange prices. for example, no City page, and nothing in its place. I have suggested already that Brownlow just turned that page over, and that it was sufficiently like what it is to-day that he passed and forgot it. I have put that suggestion to him. But he is quite sure that that was not the case. Like most of us nowadays, he is watching a number of his investments rather nervously, and he is convinced he looked for the City article.

November 10th, 1971, may have been Monday—there seems to have been some readjustment of the months and the days of the week; that is a detail into which I will not enter now—but that will not account for the absence of any City news at all. That also, it seems, will be washed out forty years from now.

Is there some tremendous revolutionary smash-up ahead, then? Which will put an end to investment and speculation? Is the world going Bolshevik? In the paper, anyhow, there was no sign of, or reference to, anything of that kind. Yet against this idea of some stupendous economic revolution we have the fact that here forty years ahead is a familiar London evening paper still tumbling into a private individual's letter-box in the most uninterrupted manner. Not much suggestion of a social smash-up there. Much stronger is the effect of immense changes which have come about bit by bit, day by day, and hour by hour, without any sort of revolutionary jolt, as morning or springtime comes to the world.

These futile speculations are irresistible. The reader must forgive me them. Let me return to our story.

There had been a picture of a landslide near Ventimiglia and one of some new chemical works at Salzburg, and there had been a picture of fighting going on near Irkutsk. (Of that picture, as I will tell presently, a fading scrap survives.) "Now that was called——" Brownlow made an effort, and snapped his fingers triumphantly. "——'Round-up of Brigands by Federal Police.'"

"*What Federal Police?*" I asked.

"There you have me," said Brownlow. "The fellows on both sides looked mostly Chinese, but there were one or two taller fellows, who might have been Americans or British or Scandinavians.

"What filled a lot of the paper," said Brownlow, suddenly, "was gorillas. There was no end of a fuss about gorillas. Not so

22

much as about that boring, but still a lot of fuss. Photographs. A map. A special article and some paragraphs."

The paper, had, in fact, announced the death of the last gorilla. Considerable resentment was displayed at the tragedy that had happened in the African gorilla reserve. The gorilla population of the world had been dwindling for many years. In 1931 it had been estimated at nine hundred. When the Federal Board took over it had shrunken to three hundred.

"*What* Federal Board?" I asked.

Brownlow knew no more than I did. When he read the phrase, it had seemed all right somehow. Apparently this Board had had too much to do all at once, and insufficient resources. I had the impression at first that it must be some sort of conservation board, improvised under panic conditions, to save the rare creatures of the world threatened with extinction. The gorillas had not been sufficiently observed and guarded, and they had been swept out of existence suddenly by a new and malignant form of influenza. The thing had happened practically before it was remarked. The paper was clamouring for inquiry and drastic changes of reorganization.

This Federal Board, whatever it might be, seemed to be something of very considerable importance in the year 1971. Its name turned up again in an article of afforestation. This interested Brownlow considerably because he has large holdings in lumber companies. This Federal Board was apparently not only responsible for the maladies of wild gorillas but also for the plantation of trees in—just note these names!—Canada, New York State, Siberia, Algiers, and the East Coast of England, and it was arraigned for various negligences in combating insect pests and various fungoid plant diseases. It jumped all our contemporary boundaries in the most astounding way. Its range was world-wide. "In spite of the recent additional restrictions put upon the use of big timber in building and furnishing, there is a plain possibility of a shortage of shelter timber and of rainfall in nearly all the threatened regions for 1985 onwards. Admittedly the Federal Board has come late to its task, from the beginning its work has been urgency work; but in view of the lucid report prepared by the James Commission, there is little or no excuse for the inaggressiveness and over-confidence it has displayed."

I am able to quote this particular article because as a matter of fact it lies before me as I write. It is indeed, as I will explain, all that remains of this remarkable newspaper. The rest has been destroyed and all we can ever know of it now is through Brownlow's sound but not absolutely trustworthy memory.

§ 5

My mind, as the days pass, hangs on to that Federal Board. Does that phrase mean, as just possibly it may mean, a world federation, a scientific control of all human life only forty years from now? I find that idea—staggering. I have always believed that the world was destined to unify—"Parliament of Mankind and Confederation of the World," as Tennyson put it—but I have always supposed that the process would take centuries. But then my time sense is poor. My disposition has always been to under-estimate the pace of change. I wrote in 1900 that there would be aeroplanes "in fifty years' time." And the confounded things were buzzing about everywhere and carrying passengers before 1920.

Let me tell very briefly of the rest of that evening paper. There seemed to be a lot of sport and fashion; much about something called "Spectacle"—with pictures—a lot of illustrated criticism of decorative art and particularly of architecture. The architecture in the pictures he saw was "towering—kind of magnificent. Great blocks of building. New York, but more so and all run together" ... Unfortunately he cannot sketch. There were sections devoted to something he couldn't understand, but which he thinks was some sort of "radio programme stuff."

All that suggests a sort of advanced human life very much like the life we lead to-day, possibly rather brighter and better. But here is something—different.

"The birth-rate," said Brownlow, searching his mind, "was seven in the thousand."

I exclaimed. The lowest birth-rates in Europe now are sixteen or more per thousand. The Russian birth-rate is forty per thousand, and falling slowly.

"It was seven," said Brownlow. "Exactly seven. I noticed it. In a paragraph."

But what birth-rate, I asked. The British? The European?

"It said the birth-rate," said Brownlow. "Just that." That I think is the most tantalizing item in all this strange glimpse of the world of our grandchildren. A birth-rate of seven in the thousand does not mean a fixed world population; it means a population that is being reduced at a very rapid rate—unless the death-rate has gone still lower. Quite possibly people will not be dying so much then, but living very much longer. On that Brownlow could throw no light. The people in the pictures did not look to him an "old lot." There were plenty of children and young or young-looking people about.

"But Brownlow," I said, "wasn't there any crime?"

"Rather," said Brownlow. "They had a big poisoning case on, but it was jolly hard to follow. You know how it is with these crimes. Unless you've read about it from the beginning, it's hard to get the hang of the situation. No newspaper has found out that for every crime it ought to give a summary up-to-date every day—and forty years ahead, they hadn't. Or they aren't going to. Whichever way you like to put it.

"There were several crimes and what newspaper men call stories," he resumed; "personal stories. What struck me about it was that they seemed to be more sympathetic than our reporters, more concerned with the motives and less with just finding someone out. What you might call psychological—so to speak."

"Was there anything much about books?" I asked him.

"I don't remember anything about books," he said. ...

And that is all. Except for a few trifling details such as a possible thirteenth month inserted in the year, that is all. It is intolerably tantalizing. That is the substance of Brownlow's account of his newspaper. He read it—as one might read any newspaper. He was just in that state of alcoholic comfort when nothing is incredible and so nothing is really wonderful. He knew he was reading an evening newspaper of forty years ahead and he sat in front of his fire, and smoked and sipped his drink and was no more perturbed than he would have been if he had been reading an imaginative book about the future.

Suddenly his little brass clock pinged Two.

He got up and yawned. He put that astounding, that miraculous newspaper down as he was wont to put any old newspaper down; he carried off his correspondence to the desk in his bureau, and with the swift laziness of a very tired man he dropped his clothes about his room anyhow and went to bed.

But somewhere in the night he woke up feeling thirsty and grey-minded. He lay awake and it came to him that something very strange had occurred to him. His mind went back to the idea that he had been taken in by a very ingenious fabrication. He got up for a drink of Vichy water and a liver tabloid, he put his head in cold water and found himself sitting on his bed towelling his hair and doubting whether he had really seen those photographs in the very colours of reality itself, or whether he had imagined them. Also running through his mind was the thought that the approach of a world timber famine for 1985 was something likely to affect his investments and particularly a trust he was setting up on behalf of an infant in whom he was interested. It might be wise, he thought, to put more into timber.

He went back down the corridor to his sitting-room. He sat there in his dressing-gown, turning over the marvellous sheets. There it was in his hands complete in every page, not a corner torn. Some sort of auto-hypnosis, he thought, might be at work, but certainly the pictures seemed as real as looking out of a window. After he had stared at them some time he went back to the timber paragraph. He felt he must keep that. I don't know if you will understand how his mind worked—for my own part I can see at once how perfectly irrational and entirely natural it was—but he took this marvellous paper, creased the page in question, tore off this particular article and left the rest. He returned very drowsily to his bedroom, put the scrap of paper on his dressing-table, got into bed and dropped off to sleep at once.

§ 6

When he awoke again it was nine o'clock; his morning tea was untasted by his bedside and the room was full of sunshine. His parlourmaid-housekeeper had just re-entered the room.

"You were sleeping so peacefully," she said; "I couldn't bear to wake you. Shall I get you a fresh cup of tea?"

Brownlow did not answer. He was trying to think of something strange that had happened.

She repeated her question.

"No. I'll come and have breakfast in my dressing-gown before my bath," he said, and she went out of the room.

Then he saw the scrap of paper.

In a moment he was running down the corridor to the sitting-room. "I left a newspaper," he said. "I left a newspaper."

She came in response to the commotion he made.

"A newspaper?" she said. "It's been gone this two hours, down the chute, with the dust and things."

Brownlow had a moment of extreme consternation.

He invoked his God. "I wanted it *kept*!" he shouted. "I wanted it *kept*."

"But how was *I* to know you wanted it kept?"

"But didn't you notice it was a very extraordinary-looking newspaper?"

"I've got none too much time to dust out this flat to be looking at newspapers," she said. "I thought I saw some coloured

29

photographs of bathing ladies and chorus girls in it, but that's no concern of mine. It didn't seem a proper newspaper to me. How was I to know you'd be wanting to look at them again this morning?"

"I must get that newspaper back," said Brownlow. "It's—it's vitally important. ... If all Sussex Court has to be held up I want that newspaper back."

"I've never known a thing come up that chute again," said his housekeeper, "that's once gone down it. But I'll telephone down, sir, and see what can be done. Most of that stuff goes right into the hot-water furnace, they say. ..."

It does. The newspaper had gone.

Brownlow came near raving. By a vast effort of self-control he sat down and consumed his cooling breakfast. He kept on saying "Oh, my God!" as he did so. In the midst of it he got up to recover the scrap of paper from his bedroom, and then found the wrapper addressed to Evan O'Hara among the overnight letters on his bureau. That seemed an almost maddening confirmation. The thing had happened.

Presently after he had breakfasted, he rang me up to aid his baffled mind.

I found him at his bureau with the two bits of paper before him. He did not speak. He made a solemn gesture.

"What is it?" I asked, standing before him.

"Tell me," he said. "Tell me. What are these objects? It's serious. Either——" He left the sentence unfinished.

I picked up the torn wrapper first and felt its texture. "Evan O'Hara, Mr.," I read.

"Yes. Sussex Court, 49. Eh?"

"Right," I agreed and stared at him.

"*That's* not hallucination, eh?"

I shook my head.

"And now this?" His hand trembled as he held out the cutting. I took it.

"Odd," I said. I stared at the black-green ink, the unfamiliar type, the little novelties in spelling. Then I turned the thing over. On the back was a piece of one of the illustrations; it was, I suppose, about a quarter of the photograph of that "Round-up of Brigands by Federal Police" I have already mentioned.

When I saw it that morning it had not even begun to fade. It represented a mass of broken masonry in a sandy waste with bare-looking mountains in the distance. The cold, clear atmosphere, the glare of a cloudless afternoon were rendered perfectly. In the foreground were four masked men in a brown service uniform intent on working some little machine on wheels with a tube and a nozzle projecting a jet that went out to the left, where the fragment was torn off. I cannot imagine what the jet was doing. Brownlow says he thinks they were gassing some men in a hut. Never have I seen such realistic colour printing.

"What on earth is this?" I asked.

"It's *that*" said Brownlow. "I'm not mad, am I? It's really *that*."

"But what the devil is it?"

"It's a piece of a newspaper for November 10th, 1971."

"You had better explain," I said, and sat down, with the scrap of paper in my hand, to hear his story. And, with as much elimination of questions and digressions and repetitions as possible, that is the story I have written here.

I said at the beginning that it was a queer story and queer to my mind it remains, fantastically queer. I return to it at

31

intervals, and it refuses to settle down in my mind as anything but an incongruity with all my experience and beliefs. If it were not for the two little bits of paper, one might dispose of it quite easily. One might say that Brownlow had had a vision, a dream of unparalleled vividness and consistency. Or that he had been hoaxed and his head turned by some elaborate mystification. Or, again, one might suppose he had really seen into the future with a sort of exaggeration of those previsions cited by Mr. J.W. Dunne in his remarkable "Experiment with Time." But nothing Mr. Dunne has to advance can account for an actual evening paper being slapped through a letter-slit forty years in advance of its date.

The wrapper has not altered in the least since I first saw it. But the scrap of paper with the article about afforestation is dissolving into a fine powder and the fragment of picture at the back of it is fading out; most of the colour has gone and the outlines have lost their sharpness. Some of the powder I have taken to my friend Ryder at the Royal College, whose work in micro-chemistry is so well known. He says the stuff is not paper at all, properly speaking. It is mostly aluminium fortified by admixture with some artificial resinous substance.

§ 7

Though I offer no explanation whatever of this affair I think I will venture on one little prophesy. I have an obstinate persuasion that on November 10th, 1971, the name of the tenant of 49, Sussex Court, will be Mr. Evan O'Hara. (There is no tenant of that name now in Sussex Court and I find no evidence in the Telephone Directory, or the London Directory, that such a person exists anywhere in London.) And on that particular evening forty years ahead, he will not get his usual copy of the *Even Standard*: instead he will get a copy of the *Evening Standard* of 1931. I have an incurable fancy that this will be so.

There I may be right or wrong, but that Brownlow really got and for two remarkable hours, read, a real newspaper forty years ahead of time I am as convinced as I am convinced that my own name is Hubert G. Wells. Can I say anything stronger than that?

Lightning Source UK Ltd.
Milton Keynes UK
UKHW010307090522
402648UK00001B/277